WELCOME DESPAIR

A Collection of Short Stories

BY

MAQUEL A. JACOB

Cover art by Roslyn McFarland
FarlandsPublishing

Published by
MAJart Works
2001 NW ALoclek Dr #211
Hillsboro, Oregon

www.majartworks.com

MORE BOOKS BY
MAQUEL A. JACOB

CORE TRILOGY
CORE OF CONFLICTION
SEEDS OF CONVITION
BONDS OF CONTRITION

CURVE OF HUMANITY
ORIGINS
SHADOWMEN OBJECTIVE
PURGE SEQUENCE

BLOOD DOCTRINE

COMING SOON

CRIPPLED EARTH
CURVE BOOK 4

CONTENTS

INTRODUCTION

I grew up on Science Fiction and Horror, my favorite genres on screen and in print, with the best stories being a combination of the two. Many of the mash-ups occurred in the late seventies to mid-nineties labeled by critics as D- rated because let's be honest. Plot? Not so much. All the same, I still enjoyed them.

When I decided to start publishing my works, there was a sense of dread to push the envelope too far so I acquired a tendency to dumb down verbiage and scale back on the violence. Now I feel the need to bring on the hurt, to embrace my dark side. Yet, I am wholly out of practice. Baby steps are required.

So, this small collection of shorts is that one level up. One step closer to my inner demon banging against my soul's cage to be unleashed. Despair is fitting for its subtlety. Not terrifying but a tad disturbing.

There is a hopelessness associated with it. Which is why if you were looking for some quasi happy ending in any of these stories, you've stepped onto the wrong trail.

Come take a journey into my version of light hearted trepidation, with a touch of gore.

TAKEN

Alec pedaled hard on his bike, opting to stand up for a few turns and ended up with a mouthful of his own hair as the wind whipped it around his face. He used a finger to pull it out, then tossed his hair back by vigorously shaking his head before looking back on his friends riding close behind.

The six of them always rode this stretch of land every Friday after studies, crossing the concrete bridge suspended over the river. On the other side was a clearing with a campground nestled against the small mountains visible to their right. He was one of the oldest at fourteen with Toby and Sean only a few months between them. Pete and Mike were thirteen and Denny was all of twelve.

At closer inspection, they looked younger than their years due to spotty availability of nutrient rich food stunting their growth. Some months were great, packed with meat and starch while others found each territory scrounging for sustenance.

Yet, they were stronger than they looked.

Traditional schooling had gone on the wayside long ago when the alien ships came abducting and killing. Still, everyone had to attend studies. Study groups were assigned to different sectors to ensure humans continued to be educated. Anyone over the age of eighteen was sent to combat training in addition.

Alec snorted.

Like we'd win.

He figured if we hadn't found a way to defeat the aliens this far into the game, it was probably a lost cause. As he saw it, humans had two primal instincts in the face of danger; fight or flight. There was only one answer when an alien ship appeared: flight. A select group of humans had tried the fight instinct and lost.

Not just any kind of defeat either. The worst kind. The kind that involved having your body torn apart before you knew what happened then left in plain sight as a reminder to the others which race was superior.

Just follow that first primal instinct: Run.

The ships came at random times of the day, sometimes just cruising along the horizon. Other times, they scanned the area for new prey to abduct. Most of the missing were never seen again but the way some came back was not a pretty sight.

The ships would appear and dump their remains by opening the cargo bay above land or water, regurgitating the pieces resembling chum enmasse falling out of the sky.

So, when halfway across, not far from the bridge, the sky above the river began to ripple, Alec's brain did the unthinkable. It became confused about which action to take. The boys screeched their bikes to a halt and watched the ripple solidify into an alien ship. Its massive oblong body gleamed in the late afternoon sunlight.

At first, Alec thought he might be hallucinating out of preconceived fear from thinking about this very thing only moments ago. But then, the familiar humming sound filled the air along with screaming from behind, making him turn his head slowly towards the source.

Toby and Mike were already lifted three feet off the ground, still on their bikes, from a whirlwind surrounding them. Toby grabbed the ledge of the bridge in a desperate attempt to not be taken. Mike didn't get that option as his body tilted backwards, legs flailing wildly in midair.

Frozen on his bike, his mind and body continuing to struggle with a decision, Alec could hear himself screaming in his head.

Grab him!

Toby let out a primal scream as his fingers snapped, broken. He watched in horror, tears stinging his eyes and in seconds Mike and Toby were sucked up through the air by an invisible vacuum into the alien ship.

More screaming.

This time from Pete who sat on his bike, hands gripping the sides of his head while tears and snot ran like a river down his face. Denny and Sean seemed in a catatonic state of terror. Alec squeezed the handle bars and his eyes tight to block out the scenery. His hands began to go numb from the pressure and he felt his whole body shake. Not able to hold it back any longer, he let out an anguished cry.

A look back up at the slow moving alien ship making its way towards the mountains, his mind suddenly made a decision and his body finally moved. Standing tall, he set one foot on the pedal and pushed down. As the bike went forward he leaned over the handle bars and set the other foot to work. He pedaled hard, reaching the three quarter mark across the bridge before he heard the other bikes coming up behind him. They passed into the clearing and Alec glanced up at the mountains with unspoken hope.

Sometimes they land.

◆◆◆

The horrible smell Toby recognized as the min- gling of blood, piss and shit. Not surprising since he had pissed himself long ago. What did surprise him was the number of bodies piled high in the small receptacle, forming a massive heap of broken human flesh. Some literally, like him.

They've been collecting.

Which meant they had gone through a good amount of humans and preparing for a dump. A new supply was needed for replacements. Toby didn't dare move. Most of his fingers were broken and a sharp pain radiated from his spine. His body was arched backwards atop a dozen others so his limited view in the dim light was upside down. An attempt to search for Mike was now out of the question, his scenarios of escape that ran through his head as they were being sucked in, dashed. He heard sob bing beneath him.

Didn't they know it was too late for that?

A door opened, spilling harsh light into the room revealing what he already knew was a sight of horrors. Blood continued to spread on the floor, creating a pool beneath the human pile. For the first time, he got to see the enemy up close and became frightened. He had expected some hideous life form but instead found two humanoid beings standing in the doorway. One was a pale bluish grey with eyes of the same hue while the other had yellowy jaundice skin and pale eyes. It shocked him more when they spoke.

"Are they all alive, still?" The blue one nodded towards the pile.

"One moment."

The yellow one pulled out a rectangular screen from his apron's front pocket and held it up. Multi colored lights swirled across its surface then faded. He stowed the device.

"Only three didn't survive. We'll have to send them to recycling."

"Hmm. The bottom ones?" The blue one inquired. "Actually, just one at the bottom is dead. The other two are somewhere in the middle."

"Well, let's drag them off so we can weed them out."

Both aliens stepped forward, reaching into the pile and pulled off bodies. The yellow one met his gaze and stopped. Toby's eyes widen, unable to control his fear.

"You want to know how we can speak your language. It's not hard to learn and we decided it worked best when giving you commands." He resumed dragging bodies out and laying them in a row outside the door.

"That one's pretty, probably a shifter."

The blue one gestured at Toby.

The yellow one came back to give Toby a closer sizing up.

"You may be right. The emperor will want this one for the playpen."

By grabbing one of Toby's arms, he pulled him off. Toby screamed from excruciating pain even though it hurt his throat. His vocal chords gave out, leaving him shuddering with tears streaming down his face.

"No need to worry. In the playpen, your body will be virtually perfect."

Out of the corner of his view, he saw the blue one pull the mangled body of a child out. Everything about its position was wrong and Mike's eyes were wide open, filled with caked blood.

"This one is no good. Most of his bones are broken. Must have happened during transport. I'm sure he didn't live long after that."

Toby squeezed his eyes shut. If he could cry more, those tears would be for Mike. Exhaustion and pain took hold of him followed by darkness. He didn't even have the energy to be angry. He was alive, for now.

◆◆◆

"Good as new."

The muffled voice sounded very close to Toby. A sharp pinching sensation subsided as a large needle nearly the size of a child's arm came into view along with a pale man in a lab coat holding it in his fist. He nodded in approval while looking down at Toby.

"She's all ready to go."

Toby tensed up. She? Quickly glancing down to confirm the man's claim, Toby found the absence of a Johnson and small mounds on a once flat chest.

Oh holy shit!

The man in the lab coat set the needle down on a nearby tray and smacked her on the thigh, the sound echoing in the chamber.

The yellow alien lifted her off the table by the shoulder and knees then set her down on both feet. He waited patiently for Toby to steady herself. No more pain. She stood stark naked staring at her body in awe for a brief moment because it was, for lack of a better word, pristine. Remembering her situation, she snapped out of it.

"We were able to create a formula that could regenerate most human tissue. If they start to break down we'll give you another round. Of course, it doesn't work if you die."

She was led out into the corridor where two other naked humans waited to be escorted. Familiar anguished faces from the collection receptacle came around the corner and marched down the adjacent hall. They were dressed in drab brown uniforms and a huge animal like alien yelled out orders.

"Move! The meal hall stops for no one. Food needs to be prepared nonstop!"

Toby eyed their own guard and he looked like the animal creature's twin. The yellow alien nudged her and she realized the others were walking. She followed in silence, observing the flurry of activity aboard the ship. As her group went further in, the corridors brightened and widened. Many of the aliens roaming around were more human in appearance. None of them looked their way. They reminded him of a royal court, which he read about in one of the salvaged book collections.

The group stopped in front of a large bay window and Toby reared back in horror. On the other side was a small white room with pristine skinned humans shackled by the neck and ankles to the floor. Most of them were young, their eyes listless. She had seen the effects of trauma many times and knew the white hair they all sported came from that.

"This is your new home, the playpen," the yellow alien announced. "If you're lucky, our ship's emperor could take a liking to you and make you his personal pet."

"How often does that happen?"

The girl who asked looked younger than Toby.

"Hmm. No human has intrigued him so far, but the offer stands until then."

"What is this?" Toby found her voice hoarse from the screaming.

"A viewing room for the emperor's pleasure. In you go."

He shoved them inside and an attendant shackled them down in record time. After making sure they were well put, the attendant exited the room and accompanied the yellow alien down the hall. As they disappeared from view, Toby looked around and his gaze was met by a young boy on his left. Intense fear exuded from him.

"Why won't they kill us?" The boy whispered. "I just want them to kill us."

Toby scanned the room.

A confined space with nowhere for any of them to run even if they weren't shackled. Shadows played along the bay window and a small group of aliens stood in front of it. The tallest one in the middle was platinum blonde with hints of yellow streaks. His demeanor and dress conveyed his importance: The ship's emperor. Toby deduced the four flanking him as servants or court appointees.

Red lights suddenly lit up along the bottom of the walls and everyone started to move randomly about in a frenzy. Before Toby knew why, the screaming started. And then he saw them. Small skinless white creatures similar to rats came scurrying out in waves across the floor, moving over them. Toby also tried to move back but the shackles stopped him a few inches from where he sat.

Teeth. Lots of them as the creatures let out small squeaks.

One of them circled around the boy next to him and began to burrow itself through his anus. Toby felt faint, the room tilting as she swayed, hearing the screams. More than that, she heard the little monsters chewing, biting; crunching.

Glancing towards the window and she saw

the gleam of ecstasy in the emperor's silver eyes. A creature ran up and she instinctively clamped her legs shut with all her might, but in vain. The thing climbed her thigh and went underneath.

She screamed even before it force its way into her and started chewing from inside. Blood spurted out of her mouth as she passed out, her vocal chords now useless.

The emperor sighed in satisfaction as he walked down the hall with his entourage. After twenty minutes of the creatures' feeding frenzy, all the toys in his playpen lay unconscious or half dead. Their bodies would heal in the next 48 hours and he decided to give them an additional two day reprieve to accommodate the new ones.

The dark haired one in particular amused him. For the first time one of his toys had actually stared him down. That one had disgust for him written all over her pretty face. He found her anguish more arousing than the whole.

"The little ones were quite hungry today, don't you think, you grace?"

"Of course they were. I demanded they be unfed for at least a week."

"Such cruelty."

"They are all my toys to do with as I please."

The emperor halted.

"Are you judging my methods?"

His entourage also stopped, shaking their heads in fervor.

"We were just admiring your deviousness."

The emperor frowned. He always made sure his toys were kept in good condition. Humans were such fragile species and many just couldn't endure the play. To him, it sounded like his court attendants suggesting he treated them poorly. He would not tolerate it.

"Explain yourself."

His attendant nervously answered.

"The mites eat through almost anything but for them to feed on organics they need to enter through an available orifice. Our study of humans tells how protective they are of their own. It corresponds with their sense of dignity."

Deep in thought, the emperor smiled. Yes, that was one reason why he did it. Stripping them of their so called dignity was a bonus in addition to watching the mites moving around under the skin of scream- ing humans. Just thinking about it made him change is mind about the reprieve.

That being said, he still found his attendant's tone offensive but decided to remedy it later. He resumed his stroll down the hall and his attendants followed in complete silence.

Four days.

That is how long Toby calculate she had been in the playpen and her hair had gone white the second day. The little white critters were allowed to munch until they exited the body hours later. Two of the prisoners, because let's face it that's what they were, had died in the process. After the mites scurried back into the walls, the dead were dragged off to the side in a corner where a compartment opened.

Sharp serrated rotary blades, four in a row, spun and the bodies were rolled in. Blood splattered on everything in the vicinity, Toby being in the zone. It coated her in a splash but she didn't move or flinch. She couldn't speak, let alone scream because her vocal chords never had time to heal even though the rest of her body did at a rapid pace. Except today.

The door opened and the yellow alien from before came in with a needle. He produced a rag from his apron and wiped blood from the right side of her abdomen.

"You seem to be having a hard time since yesterday. We have to keep you in prime condition for the emperor. This will fix you right up."

Pain seized her as the needle went through just under her ribcage and only a sharp breath come out of her instead of a cry.

"IImm. That's from the constant screaming. You should stop doing that."

Toby slowly glanced over at him and his eyes widened at the look of hatred on her face.

"Well, it's a suggestion in any case." He leaned

closer and whispered in her ear. "The emperor seems to take a liking to you. Be good and you could be in his care soon enough."

The yellow alien left the room and Toby sat stunned with a new kind of fear. Those words the first boy she met spoke echoed in her head. Death would be welcomed about now. She couldn't imagine what being the emperor's personal pet would entail and had no intention of finding out.

The emperor watched Toby with great interest and, to his own amazement, lust. He concluded it must be from human determination to survive and her refusal to submit like the others. It had been reported that she could no longer speak, the damage more severe than her internal wounds, needing more time for repair. Her eyes were not dead and listless but the hair had turned white making her more beautiful.

His attendants came advancing towards him and he realized he had forgotten the mating ceremony scheduled earlier to congratulate the couplings. He turned away from the playpen and made his way to meet them. The mites would be released in the morning to entertain him before breakfast.

❖❖❖

Of the couples recently joined, the Emperor recognized one of the brides who rejected one of his attendants at the beginning of his tenure. She laughed happily with her new mate, a member of the lowest royal court. The magistrate walked them over to him for presentation.

"Your grace, I introduce the maiden Fah and her mate, Lord Hass,"

He grimaced at how the two names resonated but smiled all the same. Stepping towards them, he pierced their stares with his own and they flinched from him.

"Such a joyous occasion. It must be exhilarating to be joined with your true mate."

His voice dripped with venom and he made no attempt to hide it. He turned to the inner deck and looked out on the mountains his ship hovered over. The river churned far below and a thought came to him. Raising his hand, he gestured for them to join him to experience the cool air.

"It fascinates me," he said as they stood near him, "how two can find one another in such short time. How did you know he was destined for you, Maiden Fa?"

The unabashed tart had the nerve to blush and smile up at Lord Hass. Research of Earth language found him intrigued by descriptive words and that one fit her perfectly.

"He was quite kind to me and felt comfortable including me in his circle not long after we met."

"Is that so?" The emperor's eyes darkened to a steely grey. "Was my attendant's offer of mating so offensive that you decided an objector to my reign suited you best?"

Maiden Fa's expression became one of surprise while Lord Hass frowned, pulling her away from the emperor. The attendant in question looked away in disappointment.

"I jest." The emperor smiled.

"Come let me congratulate you properly."

He took hold of their right hands and placed them atop each other. A soft breeze ruffled their hair.

"May your days be filled with all the wonders of mating." Then, he yanked Lord Hass forward and sent him over the ledge. His screams faded rapidly as his body fell towards the river. Loud gasps resounded and he turned to Maiden Fa.

"Now you are free to join MY court."

He addressed his attendant.

"She is yours to do as you please."

Maiden Fa stiffened, then attempted to go forth the way of her mate but the emperor back handed her, sending her right into his attendant's arms. She whimpered, her eyes pleading with her new owner, but he just glared down at her.

Being rejected by a lowly maiden at the start of his success left a deep hurt he had discussed with the emperor on the day it occurred.

"You are dismissed for the day. I am sure you need to get reacquainted."

"Thank you, your grace. I will do just that."

The emperor smiled wider as his attendant dragged the Maiden Fa by her dress collar behind him down the hall. She cried and kicked the whole way to the lift that would take them to the attendant's personal chamber.

◆◆◆

Alec caught a glimpse of something in the sky and turned his attention to it. He was pretty sure it was not a human free falling into the river, splattering into a bloody mess as it hit the surface.

So they go after their own too.

He was close to the top of the mountain where the alien ship had settled. Only a few days ago, it had dumped human remains out onto the valley floor, some tumbling down into the river. Pete, Denny and Sean had long abandoned him, coming to their senses after the second day and heading back to the compound. They called him insane before ditching him.

This did not constitute insanity.

He had finally resolved to save friends who he had known since they were babies in the makeshift camps. Survival training came in handy for his mission so he wasn't starved or dehydrated. In fact, he felt more energized than ever. In a clearing, at the base of the ship, the ramp was down and a constant flow of activity surrounded it. He brought his hands together and silently thanked fate for giving him opportunity.

Blending into the flux to be shuffled onboard was a piece of cake and when he got there, let out a sigh of relief at how busy inside. Humans in dazed despair went about their duties paying him no mind but he ducked down and moved in small intervals just in case. The corridors became more condensed as he edged in deeper.

An hour later he was searching for a weapon to defend himself and came across a lonely scythe that looked like it came from medieval times. The curved edge was forged with spikes resembling tiny teeth and the handle had raised bands of bronzed metal. A peek around the doorway where it sat, he saw a group inside the room chatting in alien tongue. He made sure no one else traveled the halls before skittering over to grab it.

Goddammnit!

Alec was no wimp but this thing was heavy. Not too heavy that he couldn't lift it but would take a lot of muscle to swing in a real fight. Up ahead, a group of high class aliens stood in front of a large bay window. The one in the middle had the most disturbing smile on his face that fear crept up him. Whatever the group was watching it seemed to be quite entertaining. As they moved away after what felt like eternity to Alec, he slinked across the wall towards the window.

Looking both ways, he dashed to the other side, hugging the wall as he crept closer. At the edge of the bay window he raised his head and took a peek.

This is wrong! This is wrong! This is wrong!

The shiny, nearly white, naked bodies were shackled like animals to the floor and most of them were either unconscious or catatonic. His focus zeroed in on a female in the center who was not moving with eyes wide open. Her skin rippled around the stomach area and he realized something was traveling inside.

As confirmation, a mound formed, bulging upwards until the skin broke and collapsed on itself. A tiny snout pushed through creating a circle of blood that spread out, staining the perfect flesh. Using its tiny teeth to take small bites, chewing between each one, the creature created a hole big enough to climb out with ease. Its belly extended from having its fill, the thing scurried away.

Bile rushed up Alec's esophagus and he couldn't stop its flow even after clamping a hand over his mouth. The vile liquid spewed forth through his fingers and dripped onto the floor. He watched the open wound on the girl start to slowly close and looked away, only to have his sights land on the female slumped against the block further in.

White hair and flawless skin be damned, he knew his best friend immediately. Toby sat lifeless, eyes half open. A pool of blood spread beneath her and Alec saw one of the rodent like things run off away from her.

Something inside of him broke.

A new kind of hatred, one he could never have fathomed, bloomed. Everything became much clearer. He wiped his mouth with his other hand and flicked the vomit off the other. The scythe weapon seemed lighter too. Boots striking the corridor caught his attention and he moved back across the hall and hid in the dark section of the corner.

A blue male alien walked right up to the console by the bay window and entered a code. He barely opened the pneumatic door when Alec mustered every bit of power he had into pushing the unsuspecting alien into the room with enough force to send him flying. Breathing hard, he went over to Toby and used his weapon to cut the shackles. To his amazement, Toby's eyes moved to stare at him.

"Let's get the fuck outta' here."

Toby only nodded and tried to assist him getting her off the floor. She was so light, like her body was empty. That made him shove the thought out of his head.

Focus.

He nearly fled out of the room, making his way back towards the way he came. His plans were dashed when a loud klaxon sounded. A large group of aliens convened up ahead. They had not seen him yet so he back tracked and coming up to the bay window found the blue alien conscious and holding down a sensor on the wall.

The two caught the other's stare for a moment before Alec noticed the alien didn't pursue due to one leg being broken the wrong way. He ran for the other side of the corridor. Further in he saw light and smelled open air.

The emperor stopped in the middle of the hall to listen at the sound of the alarms. It signaled an escapee which he found ludicrous. No one escaped his ship. Turning around he came face to face with one of his royal guards.

"Speak."

The guard bowed his head first then did as commanded.

"One of your toys has been relinquished from the playpen."

"Explain."

It took most of his resolve to not burst out in anger.

"It appears to be a rescue attempt."

The answer sounded more like a question and the emperor did not appreciate the tone.

"You are telling me that a human on this ship has decided to help his fellow man and of all things, he took one of my toys?"

"That is correct."

"Who is responsible for this?" Just as the guard was about to answer, he raised a hand to stop him. "No matter." The emperor gestured to his attendants. "Come, let's see what daft human finds themselves clever."

They returned to the corridor leading to the playpen and halfway there, the group encountered a spectacle by the observation deck. The emperor moved forward to stand in front of the small human wielding weapon while holding tight to the one toy he wanted to keep as his own. A wildness along with unwavering resolve shone in the boy's eyes and the emperor was taken aback by the same look his precious toy gave him the first time they saw each other.

◆◆◆

Alec moved back when the sick fucker who watched all delighted came in on the action. He had tried to get Toby to answer his questions but realized from Toby's gestured that she could no longer speak which pissed him off even more, so he had no qualms about cutting down the three aliens in pursuit earlier. He found his skills adequate with the alien weapon and also realized the sicko's identity from before.

"What silly game is this?"

The emperor stretched his arms wide.

"Stay away from us!"

"You are in possession of my favorite toy. I don't like when others touch my things."

"I won't let you have her! Not ever!"

Tears spilled down his face like tiny waterfalls. They were trapped with nowhere else to go. This battle was lost. A gentle breeze caressed the back of his neck and he stood straight. His gaze averted to the side where he caught a glimpse of the open observation bays. The edge of the mountains and the river were visible below.

He locked eyes with the emperor.

Clutching Toby tight, Alec turned and ran to the first opening. He leaped out into the air and twisted his body so he could see the ship recede from view. The emperor was at the ledge looking down at them. For some reason he wasn't scared.

Toby squeezed his shirt, grabbing a fist full and he looked over at her. She smiled. Alec settled himself and closed his eyes, doing the same as their bodies plummeted towards the river. He knew hitting the water at their speed would be like slamming into concrete but he didn't care. There would be nothing left of them and no more worries.

This was good.

The emperor watched the two humans free fall to their deaths with smiles on their faces and a new sense of elation filled him. He gripped the ledge with fervor.

"Intriguing." He turned to one of his royal guards. "Retrieve them before they hit."

"Both of them?"

"Oh yes," he grinned, beaming, with pleasure. "For my personal collection."

THE DEAD COMMUNITY

Reporters bustled into the office hurrying to their desks. Phones immediately started going off and the volume of voices rose to an almost unbearable decibel level. There were no cubicles to soften the din and the workstations were just shy of being too close for comfort. Stacks of papers were strewn across every surface.

Management had not approved the paperless route, still. The walls were covered with poster sized magazine covers of their best stories. Other outfits like theirs had gone digital already, their walls showing slide shows of famous articles.

Teddy Yolman sat at his workstation and leaned back with both feet propped on his own stack of notes at the edge of the desk. His laptop sat open in front of him, a blank document staring back. He had come in early to start on the ever so boring community news but his heart just wasn't in it. Local information is what he categorized as low level, low money stints.

The boss' office door whipped open causing a small wind storm. Everyone instinctively fell foward on their piles of paper but some still went flying. He stood in the doorway briefly before marching straight towards Teddy, and the look on his face told the fairly seasoned reporter that whatever he had for him was no more exciting than the one he was already working on.

"Teddy!"

The boss' voice boomed, making him wince.

He set one hand on the desk and leaned down, the weight forcing it to shift slightly. His boss was a six feet eight inches tall former college basketball player of lean muscle. His hair set neatly against the shoulders and a five day old scruff had grown on his face. The man's eyes twinkled. Teddy knew what that meant.

"Got a new story for ya'. New community popped up on the west end. Very affluent, lots of money there. Want you to go get some 411 on what kind of people they are, scope out the neighborhood." He winked as he made a fist and knocked on the desk. "Don't forget your camera." He walked off, his stride taking him halfway across in two steps. "Oh, and you'll have an escort. No one's available until late in the evening. Business types," he called back without turning around.

Teddy slid his legs off the desk and lurched forward in his chair.

"Fucker."

Closing his laptop, he got up, grabbed a notebook then headed for the doors. It was just after 9 o' clock and he hadn't eaten yet. He decided a late breakfast might get him going and cool his head in the process.

Community news was a shit assignment and he was told this would be the last one before getting promoted to yet another shit assignment; celebrity spotting. At least he could shmooze with the stars.

And, an escort?

That wasn't a rare thing, neighborhood heads wanting to show off their area, but he felt it wasn't necessary. What really got his tighty whiteys in a bunch was that the residents were too busy to make time for him until after business hours.

"Affluent my ass," he muttered to himself.

They were probably corporate workaholics.

He stepped out into the streets and crossed over to the diner. With his wages, it was the one place in close proximity where he could afford to eat. A cluster of bells clanged together above the door as he entered, then scanned for an empty booth. Finding one in the far corner out of the path of the sun's rays, he settled down for the long haul. He removed the notebook tucked under his arm and dropped it on the table, fetching the ballpoint pen from behind his ears.

"Fuck."

Teddy tapped the pen on the notebook and contemplated his life.

The outskirts of the community was like Fort Knox. A high brick wall easily over ten feet curved around the entire perimeter, blocking any outside view. At the entrance was a double black gate with a large circular insignia at the top. Teddy paced in front of the ominous gate waiting for his escort. He took a look past the gate and saw deserted cul de sacs. Not one car could be seen in the driveways. Since the sun was setting, the temperature was comfortably cool. He was glad to be half assed presentable wearing a sports jacket along with faded jeans and a t-shirt.

A sleek high end vehicle that probably costs more than his crappy one bedroom house pulled up behind his mediocre twelve year old sedan and a young man exited it. He also wore jeans and a t-shirt but for some reason looked better dressed than him. The man removed a pair of expensive sunglasses from his face and Teddy got a glimpse of startling grey eyes before the sun moved away, darkening them. His hair was coiffed in big waves just above his shoulders, circa the 1990's.

"Mr. Yolman." He raised a hand to shake Teddy's and he took it. "I'm Mikal."

"Thanks for coming to show me around."

"Not a problem. Sorry for the late hour. We like to unwind after a long day of doing business."

Mikal went to the passenger side of his car and opened the door.

"Please, hop in. You can leave your car here."

He saw his hesitation. "it's perfectly safe."

Teddy got in and felt the luxury right off the bat. The seat conformed to his body and there was plenty of leg room. Every inch of the interior was spotless, making him realize how much of a slob he was. He tried not to touch anything for fear of marring the surfaces with his fingerprints.

Mikal backed up the car and pulled up to the gate, presenting a keycard that he held in front of the indiscriminate box located on a pole by the curb. The black gates slowly swung open, hardly making a sound as it allowed the car to drive through.

Observing the landscape, a creepiness went through Teddy. There were no lights on in the houses they past even as dusk fell on the community, making everything look dull and grey. Mikal maneuvered the car into a parking spot in front of the community center.

They both got out and a crow screeched into the air. Teddy flinched and ducked for no reason, his eye sight landing on the damnable creature as it readjusted its position on a rooftop.

"Really?"

Shouting at the bird he stood back upright and Mikal raised an eyebrow.

"Let's go. We have a meeting with our neighborhood head."

"There's people here? Cuz, it looks deserted to me. What's going on? Am I being punked?"

Mikal frowned at him.

"Which question do you want answered?"

Teddy reeled back at the remark and reevaluated his situation. He was in an unknown place with a total stranger.

"I am so sorry, please forgive me. It's been an unproductive day so far."

"Sure." Mikal put his sunglasses back on. "Come."

They walked a few blocks then stopped at one of the plain cookie cutter homes. Up close, he could see the craftsmanship of the build. A much higher stan- dard than the other so called affluent neighborhoods he had covered over the years. Neither he nor Mikal had rang the bell yet the door swung open to reveal a woman in a maid uniform. She didn't smile or even speak, just gestured for them to enter the home. Mikal went in first and Teddy followed.

Inside was huge compared to what the outside conveyed. Floor to ceiling windows were on either side of the house, explaining why he didn't notice them from the front. The furniture was immaculate and very old world expensive looking. Teddy thought twice about sitting down on the white sofa. A soft clearing of the maid's throat made him realize he had stopped in the middle of the foyer gawking. She raised a hand towards the hallway behind her.

Along the walls were custom framed artwork. He could swear one of them was famous, possibly procured at the recent auction he heard about. At the end of the hall were double doors that the maid used both hands to slide open. Moving away from the entrance, she allowed them to pass her. Teddy whistled at the crystal decanter surrounded by smaller drinking glasses on a silver platter.

"Mr. Yolman."

You know that uber rich distinguished gentleman who makes people feel inferior?

That's what went through Teddy's head as he looked over and saw who had spoken. He felt the presence of true money. All those socialites and their asshole corporate husbands had nothing on this guy.

"I am Sir Chattham Gallaher, but here in the States I am just a business man. Please, call me Mr. Gallaher." The man smiled, showing gleaming white teeth.

"It's a pleasure to meet you, sir."

"I apologize for the lateness, but we like to wind down after work here."

"Yeah, so I've heard. The place looked kind of dead. Didn't know if I was being punked or something."

He let out a little laugh but no one else joined in, making him feel awkward.

"Please, sit. Do you like scotch?"

Sir Gallaher pointed to the crystal decanter and the maid expertly poured two glasses.

"Sure do. It's an occupational must."

Teddy turned to see Mikal still wearing his sunglasses, standing in the doorway as he leaned on the frame. He raised an eyebrow and glanced at Sir Gallaher.

"Mikal is not much of a drinker when it comes to alcohol. He likes more exotic fare."

"Whatever floats your boat." Teddy relieved the glass of scotch from the maid and raised it in the air. "Cheers."

Sir Gallaher did the same and took a small sip while Teddy downed the contents of his glass in one shot. He watched the man set his glass down on the coffee table next to him and temple his fingers.

"I'm curious as to how you view your occupation, Mr. Yolman. Is it fulfilling?"

"Hell no," Teddy scoffed. "This is my last community assignment before I get promoted to celebrity watch."

"Is that your goal?"

Sir Gallaher actually frowned at him.

"Not by a long shot. I figure I do that for another year or so and then they'll start giving me the good stuff."

"Really? So your life is not very productive or fulfilling these days?"

"You know, I actually said those exact words to Mikal just before we came here. Sometimes I like to skip town for a while to get away from the rat race."

"So no one would think anything odd if you," Sir Gallaher tilted his head upward, "took a sudden vacation?"

Teddy snorted.

"My boss would probably thank the Gods he wouldn't have to put up with me."

Silence filled the room and Teddy became aware of what he just said. He remained calm and sat back against the loveseat. Red flags went off in his head like confetti. Mikal standing behind him was now quite creepy.

"I ask because it would be unprofessional of you to not take at least a week to study our community. We can set you up with one of our not so busy residents."

The hell you say? I'm no dummy! Teddy thought to himself, trying to keep his breathing even.

"Ahh, but you're no dummy." That made Teddy's heart skip a beat. "If you want to take a tour of the neighborhood, by all means do so." Sir Gallaher smiled wider. "At your own risk of course." Mikal pushed himself off the doorframe. "Give him a good head start, Mikal."

"Of course, my lord."

He turned to Teddy. "Run."

No one had to tell him twice.

Teddy bolted for the front door like a bat out of hell. He had no idea what was in store but waiting to find out was not an option. Outside, daylight was clinging on, grey skies looming above. He thanked the heavens for not bringing the night while he was inside the house. Then he noticed how different the area appeared. Hints of color could be seen in various places where night lights flickered on. The community was coming alive.

He ran to the left towards the giant black gates, trying to gauge the distance and found he was much farther in than he thought. By the time he got there it would be dusk. Out of the corner of his eye he saw movement in a nearby alleyway and stopped in his tracks. A pair of legs were being dragged across, leaving a murky dark trail as they went. His head snapped up in fear and he forced his own legs to move. Whatever was about to go down he wanted no part of.

Scaling a house, he climbed onto the roof to scan the streets. Not a soul could be seen but he knew someone was out there dragging a bloody body. All kinds of crazy scenarios came to him. Maybe they were cannibals. They could be a cult doing human sacrifices. He remembered Mikal putting his sunglasses back on even though the sun's brightness had long diminished. Hell, they could be vampires for all he knew, which was stupid because there was no such thing. Getting back down to ground level he dropped into the adjacent alleyway.

"But something like that."

Teddy nearly jumped out of his skin as he whipped around to find Mikal standing behind him. The sunglasses were off and those grey eyes almost glowed in the dark patch where the two men stood. His tongue fell out from between his lips and licked the entire perimeter of his mouth. It was the longest tongue Teddy had ever seen in his life and it forked at the tip.

"It's no fun if you don't take the chase seriously."

Someone started screaming.

Teddy ran further down the alleyway and out into the open before realiz- ing he was the one doing it. He had always made jokes about grown men screaming like bitches in movies and now he understood. Clamping a hand over his mouth to muffle the sound, he made a beeline for the gate.

Cell phone!

Teddy took his hand from his mouth and nearly laughed. Reaching into his jacket, he pulled out his cell phone and tapped the screen to wake it up. He dropped his speed to a jog and tapped the keypad icon.

A thought came to him. If he dialed 911, what would he say? Calling the boss man would be a lesson in futility. Who should he call? It hit him. He was on his own.

There would be no miraculous rescue from some outside source.

"Exactly."

This time the maid came up right in front of

him and snatched the phone from his hands. In the blink of an eye she was gone with his only link to the outside. Stunned, he halted in the middle of the street. How fast were they? What are they? Can he really get away? He took another longing look at the gate that seemed too far away. The sun was setting further down into the horizon.

Not yet!

"I'm not giving up!" Teddy yelled up at the sky.

"Good," Mikal answered from close by.

Teddy took off like a bullet down the deserted street and was glad he went to the gym three times a week. If anything, he could last a couple of hours. That was plenty of time to get to the gate. Just as he passed a mailbox, a little girl with teeth exposed chomped down at his swinging arm, missing by a hair. He caught the glowing grey eyes and sharp pointy fangs in the split second it took him to out-run her.

Holy Shit!

Up ahead to his right was a trio bent over the bloody legs and he finally saw that was all there was. The rest of the body was nowhere to be found. The three men glanced over at him and smiled, showing their pearly white fangs. If not vampires, then what the hell were they? His legs continued to carry him towards his destination. Stopping meant death.

Four of them, two on each side, came charging at him and he nearly skidded to a stop but instead did a sharp pivot, detouring into another alleyway. He got on top of another roof and watched them stand below waiting patiently for him to come back down. A presence was close by him so he slowly turned to his left. Mikal was kneeling on the roof next to him also observing the four.

"You're getting a kick out of this aren't you?" Teddy balled his fists. "Knowing damn well a human is no match for you."

"True, but we like to let them think they can at least try."

Mikal grabbed him by the neck and next thing he knew they were on the ground. His escort let him go and got up, stepping a few feet away.

"I want to eat you," Mikal announced.

Teddy felt the blood drain out of him.

Cannibals. His first guess was right.

"Wrong."

"Did you just?"

"Read your mind? Yeah."

"All this time?" Mikal nodded. Teddy became light headed.

"I'm lonely."

"What?" Teddy was now confused.

"Everyone needs a companion in life."

"Then get a fucking pet!"

Mikal smiled. "I'm trying."

Teddy didn't think, his body moved on its own knowing a bloodthirsty thing with a human face pursued him. The gate loomed ahead and his former child self who had a knack for getting over and around obstacles took over, clambering up the wall and flipping onto the other side. He jumped down onto the street and stared up at it. Backing away towards his car, he held up a middle finger.

On the opposite side Mikal nonchalantly walked up to the gate then leapt onto the top of the wall, cock- ing his head to one side. Teddy moved back faster, fumbling in his pocket for the keys.

"I can't let you go."

Mikal's eyes glowed silver in the near dark.

"Aw Shit!"

Before he could push the key fob to open the car doors, his body was yanked forward giving him a good view of the sky while being tossed over the gate. He landed in the center of the main street with Mikal holding fast to his jacket collar.

"You should stay here with me."

"Why are you doing this? Why me?"

Mikal lifted him up by the neck and opened his mouth wide. Moisture glistened, dripping from ivory fangs as he took a huge bite into Teddy's shoulder blade, barely missing the carotid artery. An attempt to scream only caused him to choke on his own blood.

Mikal's voice spoke inside his head.

"You seemed miserable with your life. I watched you for weeks before asking permission to approach

your company for a review."

"…Can't … keep….missing…will search."

Teddy had a hard time forming words. A kind of numbness went through his body, the pain ceasing.

Neurotoxin?

Mikal disengaged and licked the gaping wound almost lovingly.

"But you said yourself, no one would miss you. And even if they do search, they'll find you safe and sound. Once you're turned, I will be able to eat off you for eternity because your body will regenerate in mere days. Doesn't that sound exciting? You'll never die."

Teddy's eyes went wide, understanding those words and came to the conclusion this was much worse than terror. He would rather die than become a walking pet doubling as snack food.

"No you don't. You want to live. And I'll take good care of you."

Mikal's fangs tore into him again, this time below the ribcage, ripping out part of his guts. He watched his own blood fly out of him and splash back down. Some of his intestines hung out of Mikal's mouth while he chewed, his eyes drunk with ecstasy as he savored each morsel. The last thing Teddy saw before losing consciousness was Mikal tossing his key fob to the maid who got into his car and eased it through the gate.

AND NOW FOR
SOMETHING
A LITTLE
BIZARRE

HUNTERS DELIGHT

Cars sped down the highway at well above the posted limit causing a back draft of dirt and polluted air. Adam stepped further away from the road and coughed. Particles of debris flew into his already dirty blonde hair. Over the past month, it had grown out to sit just above his shoulders in slight waves. He rustled it with his fingers, dislodging some of the dirt and sighed.

Wearing jeans, an old concert tee and cross trainer sneakers, he was comfortable in the late afternoon summer weather. Temperatures were mild for the season this year and he thanked the Gods for it. The expensive back pack he carried had the bare minimum necessities for keeping up hygiene and appearance. At the rest stop a few miles back, he used a disposable razor to get rid of his week old scruff.

A month ago felt like eternity. The company he worked for got hit hard leaving everyone in a lurch. Feds came bursting in, locked and loaded, yelling while the suits brandished warrants and started ransacking the place. In the aftermath weeks later, it was announced that all accounts were frozen, everyone's. And there seemed to be no sympathy for the office workers like him who got caught up in the mess unaware.

With no money to pay for rent, his car or eating, he lost everything. Having nothing but the few belongings on his back, he set out on a hitchhiking and begging adventure. In a month he had gone through four states, doing odd jobs for cash under the table. Another vehicle came along and as he turned to raise a thumb it came thundering pass, whipping his hair back. Gravel and dirt sprayed his face.

"Shit!"

He spit out the foul matter and wiped his mouth with the back of his hand.

The monstrous truck disappeared down the highway but he could still make out the numerous gun racks and giant floodlights.

"Fucking rednecks," he muttered to himself.

Brushing off his pants, he stepped back onto the edge of the highway and put his thumb out again. A sedan slowed down to a crawl and stopped next to him. The driver rolled down the passenger window with a touch of a button and leaned over.

"Saw you got the wind knocked outta ya' by that big one up there."

"Yeah, they were going pretty fast."

"Well hop in. I can get you to the next stop, if that helps."

"That would be great. Thanks."

Adam slid into the passenger seat and leaned

his head back. Both arms lay limp on either side of him.

"Been trekking long today?"

"Past two days. Only thing saving my feet are the tennies."

"Then you need a rest. Relax. We should be there in about three hours. I'll wake ya"

"Thanks again," Adam mumbled as he fell asleep.

◆◆◆

A jolt up his spine woke him up as the sedanrolled over rough terrain before smoothing out on black top. The truck stop had a few vehicles parked in its lot, one being the behemoth that nearly creamed him earlier. His eyes felt sticky and he used a finger to rub the gunk out of the corners. There was a throbbing in is legs like tiny needles probing.

"Here we are," the driver piped up.

He parked the sedan at a gas pump and jumped out. Adam felt old in contrast and eased out of the passenger door at a snail's pace. His body just didn't want to cooperate. Looking at the grey sky he again thanked the weather Gods for the cooling off. After a moment, he stretched his arms high above his head and heard a satisfying crackle pop from his back.

"Do you need some gas money?"

The older man shook his head.

"Thanks for offering but I got this. You save your money for some good truck stop food. It's the best on the road."

"Well, thanks again. Drive safe."

As he got halfway to the diner doors, the man yelled out, "You be safe out here."

Adam gave him a thumbs up and continued on into the diner. Dim yellow light spread sparse gave the place a dinginess only found in Middle America. Old leather booths and wooden bar stools that screamed hand carved waited for a tired trucker's butt to land on them. An old couple, a group of college kids prob- ably on a summer road trip and a handful of big rig drivers were present. Off in the back by the pool table was an eclectic bunch. Two corporate guys, a bear of a man, two rednecks and a tall well-built woman with huge knockers.

He sauntered over to the bar where a couple of truckers nursed their pints of draft beer and slid onto the clackety bar stool. Dropping his sack on the floor by his feet, he let out a sigh. The barmaid slapped a hand on the bar in front of him to get his attention.

"Whatcha' havin'?"

Her voice had an air of irritation.

"Got whiskey?"

She snorted and walked off to pull a bottle off the shelf. On the way back, she snatched a glass which got slammed down between his outstretched arms. The whiskey was poured, the bottle raised up high above the glass without a drop splashing. She set the bottle down next to the glass.

"Help yourself after this."

The barmaid went to serve the other end of the bar.

"Uhh, thanks."

"Anybody who orders whiskey this early must be having some kind of day," a male voice spoke.

To the left of him was one of the corporate looking guys from the back. In his hand was a huge billfold, making Adam envious. He too used to carry that much just for show. The man nodded down at his backpack.

"Hitching?"

"Yep." Adam took a swig of whiskey and winced.

"How long?"

"About a month or so."

The man whistled. "Hard times, huh?"

"Corporate drama. Went belly up in Federal corruption flames."

"And all the small fries got caught in the fire."

"You got it." Another swig and this one felt like acid burning his esophagus.

"Come on back and join us. We'll buy you a few."

Adam glanced over his shoulder.

"No way. Your friends look like the type who would gouge my eyes out if I looked cross eyed at their lady."

The man smiled and let out a snort.

"Trust me, that's no one's lady."

"Tough cookie, huh?"

"Oh, and then some." He straightened up. "I'm Greg. Come on. No reason for you to drink alone."

He waved a fifty at the barmaid who sashayed quickly down to them.

"Another round and whatever he's having too."

"You got it, big spender," she replied.

Two hours later and Adam knew he was drunk as hell. With four beers and the shots he lost count of, there was no way he could thumb it the rest of the way into the next state. He had also learned the group was a hunting party and that giant truck was theirs. Big tits never spoke a word but made eye contact with him several times.

"Ever been hunting?"

The dude named Clint asked it with a disturbing gleam in his eye.

"Nope. I'm a true blue city boy."

"That braves the road with nothing but a sack and hitches cross country?" Greg shook his head. "Not very city boy behavior."

"You should come on with us," Clint suggested. "Show you a thing or two and you'd eat good. Ain't that right, Robbie?"

Big tits locked eyes with him and Adam felt

his groin tighten. A longing swept through those eyes and then it was gone.

"I'd like that."

The voice that came out was deep but subtle like that famous movie actress who was known for her deep rasp. It sent chills through him, creating a fervor of lust. He silently chastised himself for thinking about going the distance. This scenario was something out of an old slasher film where one of the guys really was her man and just waiting for him to make a move.

"Then it's settled!" The big bear sized man who called himself Jess threw an arm around his back and put him in a light choke hold. As the tallest of the group, at six foot five and weighing nearly three hundred pounds, he felt like a brick wall. "Let's have some fun!"

He started to protest but to no avail. Realizing he had no chance of refusing, Adam accepted another round of shots and tried to enjoy himself.

◆◆◆

Sunlight and the jostling motion of the truck jarred him awake and he found himself lying on the cabin floor with his head in big tits lap. Long fingers caressed his head and it felt good. He gave a small sniff and turned his head to the side, getting comfortable.

"Uh oh, I think he likes you," Greg quipped.

Adam frowned, then remembered where he was and who with. He sat abruptly, wiping his eyes. There wasn't much room to stretch his legs but he gave it a shot.

"I wasn't trying to hit on her or anything." Everyone except Robbie snickered. "What? I mean it. No offense, Robbie, but I like to be cautious. Just in case."

"In case what?"

"One of these guys really is your boyfriend."

More snickering.

"They're not. No worries."

"Coming up to a patch of woods. Get yer balls in order," Clint called out. "Get us in close, Dave."

Dave maneuvered the truck onto the trail and slowed down.

At a clearing, they all dismounted from the truck. While he stood admiring the greenery, the rest of them brought out hunting gear. Some time goes by and he starts to wonder why none of them offer him a weapon. As if reading his mind, Clint slaps him on the back.

"Newbies shouldn't handle dangerous toys. That's how they get hurt. Just follow our lead and you should be okay."

"Got it."

"Good. Let's go a huntin'."

Smack!

Another bug had bitten Adam in the leg and along with his hand both were now red from him constantly trying to swat them away, making them angry instead. The group had split off and he was with bear man Jess. Where the others stalked their prey in stealth, he went thundering into the woods like a wild beast. Adam steered clear of him.

Twigs snapping caught their attention and bear dude stopped mid stride, a crazed expression on his face. He turned like a robot towards the sound of an actual bear barreling out of the trees, scaring him stiff. But not Jess.

Jess let out a loud battle cry and launched himself at the animal. A wrestling match ensued between man and beast. Jess got his bearings and brought the bear down while pulling his serrated knife out from his back holster. With a viciousness Adam had never witnessed before, he used the knife to saw into the bears neck, all the while yelling and grunting.

Horrified, Adam bolted out of the woods and made a beeline for the truck, a good two miles away. He was in decent shape and sprinted the whole way. Reaching his destination, he used one hand for leverage on the truck bed as he tried to catch his breath. His heartrate settled and he had immediate cotton mouth. He looked up over the edge and saw the large steel coolers. One of them had to have the beers in it.

Climbing up, he popped the latch on the first one and saw all the butchered meat. It was a huge haul as far as he could tell. Each cut was neatly packaged in vacuum sealed plastic bags with a small tiny letter in the corner for identification. Just as he was about to close it, a piece caught his eye. The long piece still attached to the bone seemed awfully familiar. Over the years, he had seen many pictures of quartered bucks and this was not any deer leg he knew of. Now, he was no surgeon but he had taken anatomy back in college and knew a human calf when he saw one.

He slowly shut the lid, relatched it and jumped off the truck. A sharp pain spread across his face from his eyes trying to bulge out their sockets, causing a headache. Going around to the cabin, he opened the door, retrieved his backpack and instinct took over. Running like a crack whore on fire, his stride awkward, he wondered how far away from them he could get on foot. The inside joke he made to himself about being in an old slasher flick came back with a vengeance.

"Stupid, stupid, stupid!"

He should have said no thanks at the truck stop and found a ride later.

Twigs crackling in the distance behind him let Adam know the hunting party was on his trail. Even with the huge head start, he couldn't get away fast enough. Deeper into the woods he went, hoping for salvation. To his right, a glimpse of a structure caught his attention and he ran towards it for a better look.

A shed.

The wooden building had faded in color from being exposed to the environment, splotched with shades of grey and rust. A few tall weeds grew around the edges at the base but the most important feature he noticed was the unlocked door. Rusty metal plates held on to an old bolt that lot its usefulness long ago. Drenched in sweat, Adam wrenched the door open and ran in.

Inside was huge. Directly in front of him was wide open space stopping shadow further in before a row of stalls. On either side of him were shelves, more stalls and piles of hay. His mind went through options, a virtual rolodex of ideas flipping at high speed.

Snap!

Hearing the break of wood just outside forced him to act. The piles of hay were stacked inside a wooden stall on his right. There was no visible entrance but he went to it anyway. Some of the boards had worn loose so he jiggled one of them up enough for him to fit through. He settled down into the hay, burrowing into it to blend in, as the door swung open and Greg stood haloed by the passing sunlight.

Three of the hunters made their way into the shed, scanning the place for him. Adam wanted to squeeze his eyes shut but refused to lose sight of them in case he had to make a move. Still outside was Big Tits, Clint and bear dude standing guard.

Each one took a gander checking out the vicinity probably hoping he would come out from the back.

No chance.

He may be a little green in the whole being chased department but he was no dummy. Years of movie watching taught him a few things. Dave stopped in the center, cocking his head up to one side, listening. After what felt like eternity, his head straightened and his gaze landed right on the pile of hay. He just nodded and Greg did the same.

"Come on out of there, now. No need to turn this into a situation. Good ol Jess here just gets a little overzealous when he goes in for a kill. Nothing to run away from." Greg walked slowly towards him as he spoke.

Bullshit! Adam screamed in his head.

"Just grab him," Bear dude Jess yelled and pushed his way in heading for him.

The pump action of a shotgun drew their attention and everyone stopped. From his view in the hay, he saw an old couple in their pajamas clinging to each other, the man holding the weapon a mere foot away from Clint's face. Big Tits had a curious look on that pretty face: One that frightened him. Dave kept his stare on him, never wavering.

"Now, I don't know what you huntin' for out here but I need y'all to vacate my property."

The old man's voice and stance was solid. He meant business. Bear dude made a loud howl and did a quick pivot, going for the couple. He got almost within strike range when the other two hunters along with Clint restrained him.

"Hold on there, big guy," Clint warned. "Let's not cause a fuss." He eyed Big Tits who took hold of the large man's arms, pulling them behind. Clint addressed the couple. "We're real sorry for disturbing you and trespassing. We been out hunting and didn't know there was anyone living this far out"

"Well, now ya' do."

"Come on people, let's go."

Dave finally turned away and left out the barn along with Greg. Jess was still chomping at the bit ready to tear the old couple apart. It took four from the group to literally pull him away back towards the way they came. When he couldn't hear them anymore and the old couple seemed to be satisfied with their distance, the old man spoke again.

"That means you too. I know you're in there hiding but this ain't it. I'll give you about twenty minutes then come back shooting if you not out."

With that, the man lowered his shotgun and the couple left. Adam realized he had been shaking as he pulled himself through the loose board back out onto the barn's floor.

A coolness at his crotch let him know he had pissed himself.

No shame in that.

He was surprised the backside of his shorts weren't stained as well. Brushing off his ass, he made his way on shaky legs to the door and out into the open air.

◆◆◆

Two days on the run found him haggard but thoroughly pissed off for being so naïve. Because he feared being spotted by the hunters, his route into the next state over entailed off beaten paths and shady guys in trucks. One even tried to cop a feel while he was asleep in the passenger seat. His clothes were worse for wear, dirty and oh so aromatic. Hygiene always being at the top of the list, he would forgo it for now in lieu of the life threatening situation.

Flickering lights up ahead made him squint, the brightness hurting his eyes. Elation came over him as a rundown motel in the middle of nowhere came into view. As he got closer, the price flashed across the half working sign;

39.95 A Night! Vacancy

"My kind of price."

Half an hour later, he was palming a room key and getting some necessities from the small makeshift convenience rack. Inside his room, he laid out the goods: toothpaste, a comb and the most important item of all, a razor. He sat on the bed and laid down for a while contemplating his predicament. With a heavy sigh, he slid off the bed and went into the bathroom to take a shit, shower and shave.

All cleaned up and feeling refreshed, Adam sauntered out of bathroom naked and stood in the doorway. His equilibrium swayed, forcing him to stumble towards the bed and slam into it. Face down, knocked out cold, is how he ended the rest of the day.

The sound of doors slamming and people talking jarred him out of his deep slumber some ten hours later. Still in a supine position, he focused on the clock by the bed and saw it was past noon. A chill ran up his spine and he became aware of his nakedness. He sat up and grabbed his back pack off the floor, digging in to find his clean clothes at the bottom.

Once dressed, he went out to the main office and bought a light breakfast consisting a protein bar, some chips, a banana and orange juice that he took back to his room. He watched about an hour of television then repacked his sack for another long trek. Checkout was at three so there was no rush. Laying back on the bed, his eyes closed, he decided to chill for a bit.

When he woke up, the sun was setting and he jumped up in a panic only to come face to face with Clint. A quick scan of the room and he saw the whole hunting party in his room making themselves comfortable.

Instinct kicked in yet again with no hope in sight as he bolted into the bathroom and tried to barricade himself. Thoughts of his stupidity were short lived. The door shudder from a heavy hit on the other side before the second impact busted the door off its hinges and wide open. Adam went sailing across the floor, hitting the side of the tub. Before he could get back up, Dan came in with something that resembled shiny entrails dangling from his hand and shoved it in his face.

Adam noticed they had all donned face masks just as the scent hit him. Looking more closely at the thing in front of him, he reared back in horror. Clint smiled while leaning against the door jam. Behind him by the bed was Big Tits stripping down.

"That there is an awesome piece of a prize. It's from a species fairly new that we found out about and decided to use for fun. First, we find one that's just recently given birth and separate it from its young. Then we cut the milk sacs and ovaries out, making sure to keep them intact and together."

Milk leaked from the nipples of the skinned animal's sacs and the sweet cloying scent intensified, making his body feel like gelatin.

Trying to keep himself conscious proved a chore. Dan removed the mutilated carcass from his view and Adam slumped against the edge of the tub.

In his blurred vision, he saw big tits come

towards him. A cock bigger than his own bounced erect between those thighs and Adam caught on to the jokes on the truck.

"Now, Rob here really likes you so he's gonna' have a little personal time with you for a bit."

Clint moved to let Rob in the bathroom.

"Make him like it."

Rob stood over him then flipped him over so that half his body leaned over into the tub's basin. He felt his pants being removed and knew what was about to happen. His voice seemed to not work so all the screaming he did was in his head. A slimy, sticky sub- stance was spread around the rim of his anus then pressure. Surprisingly, there was minimal pain due to his slacked body muscles. Still, he cried tears of anger and shame.

"How is it, Rob?"

Clint peeked around the sink.

"Really good. I'm going to be a while."

"Well, we'll leave you to it. Let us know when you're done."

As Clint and Dan left the bathroom, Dan stopped at the door and turned.

"He's going to make a great hunt."

"Making us run around for two days, you bet your ass, he will."

"More like HIS ass," Jess the bear dude snorted.

Clint nodded then continued to head out.

"It's alright," Rob sighed into his ear.

"I'll take good care of you until then."

Rob didn't miss a stroke as he spoke, adding to Adam's deteriorating mental state. He lay like a ragdoll being violated, wishing for salvation that he knew would never come. For the first time in two months, he realized he should have just stayed in the city and waited out the federal investigation's outcome. Being fucked out of his money was now trivial compared to what he was enduring at the moment. After what seemed like an eternity in hell, the numbing agent starting to wear off, he heard Rob speak again.

"Aww, damn it."

The awful feel of hot semen filling up his anal canal caused an involuntary convulsion and Adam violently threw up in the tub. One of Rob's hands caressed the top of his head as more spewed out.

Footsteps sounded near the doorway and Clint's voice piped up.

"Couldn't go the distance this round, huh? Well, better clean him up and get him out of here. Check out is about over and we don't want any incidents."

Rob leaned over him and turned on the shower. Dazed and feeling the first signs of pain in his ass, he watched the vomit go down the drain. When it was all clear, Rob eased him over the ledge and into the needles of water that pelted his skin even through the shirt. Still naked, Rob removed it for him then grabbed the soap.

He washed him gently, almost motherly. Adam shuddered seeing the pink water running off the tip of Rob's cock, knowing it was his blood.

His body wouldn't do what he wanted due to the lingering numbness so he just flopped all over the place. Rob got a good grip under his arms and hauled him back onto the bed. Dan pulled some clothes out of a store bag and set them on the edge.

"Figured you may want some new clothes. Those in that sack have seen better days."

While Rob redressed before helping him into the new duds, Clint came and sat beside him.

"See, we like to hunt, is all. Don't matter the prey. But, for the two legged kind, we like to make it a bit more entertaining. We release you in the hunting grounds butt ass naked before dawn and you have until daybreak. If we don't catch you by then, well, we treat you to a nice breakfast and some rest then we try again. Sounds like a pretty good deal, right?"

"Last guy lasted almost a week. I think he kind of gave up in the end, though. Broke Rob's heart. He was a bit disappointing. I got a feeling you're special."

Adam felt his eyes go wide remembering the butchered human pieces in the cooler. Rob loomed over him.

"You don't want to die, I know. Don't worry, when we catch you I'll make sure it's painless."

Adam Hunting Season had begun.

Clint let out a loud whistle, the act raising his long mustache above his upper lip. He scratched the front of his camouflage jacket, digging in so he could feel it.

"Look at that beauty! Shit, Dave, you're a damn good shot for an accountant."

Dave just stood next to him and nodded, crossbow resting on one shoulder, beady steel blue eyes focused ahead.

"The buck ain't half bad either," Clint snorted as he leaned his head to the side and spit out his chew juice.

In the quiet clearing with morning only a couple of hours old, the two men stood alongside the rest of their group in a semi-circle around two corpses on the ground. One, a healthy four point buck on its side bleeding out while the muscles ceased to twitch. The other, a naked white male with skin pale from the cold and loss of blood.

Both had an arrow protruding out of them. Compared to the buck, the man had the worse injury. The arrow had gone through the back of his head, its tip protruding out from his right eye.

Robbie went forward and squatted down next to the dead man for a closer inspection. Clint whipped out an old school disposable camera.

"Dang it, Rob! Move them things out the way so I can get a decent shot."

Rob looked back, seeing the camera already positioned to take it. Giving Clint an uninterested stare, he moved over to the left out of frame. The large breasts jiggled slightly up and down.

Jess whacked Dave on the back, making him tilt forward a bit.

"We've some good eating for next week now."

Using two fingers, Robbie brushed the matted hair from the dead man's face.

"Aww, you had fun with that one, huh?"

Clint went over to rest a hand on his head.

"He made it worth my while if that's what you mean." Robbie's tenor voice was like velvet.

"Well, hell, you can't blame him for fighting so hard after luring him in with those giant titties only to whip out your Johnson and ream him."

"Hmm." Robbie stood.

The two hunters on opposite sides of them produced large black tarps and commenced to bagging their bounty. Not far away from the clearing sat the tank sized truck with multiple rifle racks and steel storage boxes in the bed.

Securing the corpses with heavy rope, the cleanup crew grabbed hold of the ends and dragged the haul towards the vehicle. Rob stared down at the human shaped bundle bumping along the foliage, a tiny smirk on his face. Clint came up behind him.

"Ready to go hunting for a new toy next round?"

"Sure."

"Too bad we haven't found your beau, Adam, yet. He's a slick one."

"We'll find him," Robbie said softly.

"Glad you're having fun, kiddo. Beats working in a warehouse for shit salary don't it?" Robbie nodded. "Come on, gonna' be a long night of butchering that meat."

"Let's find camp so we can get the good stuff harvested and be on our way in a couple of days. We can deliver the remains when we come across a hospital or some medical place."

"Only right," the big man replied.

"We're not monsters," Dave whispered in agreement.

NOW FOR A LITLE SOMETHING
SHORT AND SWEET

A PLOT GONE AWRY

There were times when the changer thought his appearance alone gave away his origin. Relliants were a race of alien warriors stranded on Earth, scattered about in a world where society made them easy targets for malcontents who took it upon themselves to eradicate the planet of so called evil.

The Relliant's didn't help themselves by refusing to conform to human attire, still insisting on wearing their battle suits. Times like these made the changer nervous even though he was born and raised on Earth. His friends would turn on him; call him an alien freak and a traitor, if they knew the truth. The city was hostile tonight and that meant trouble.

Entering a multimedia store, he headed for the music section to browse the thrash genre. It was safer in here than on the streets and he might find some- thing good. As he progressed further into the store he caught his reflection in one of the mirrored columns.

The black wavy hair and flawless facial features were a basic trait of his race but his eyes were not black pupil on black iris like the pure bloods who attacked anything with a pulse. Instead they were a deep green that pierced you even in the night. The tell-tale signs of genetic mutation due to the fact that his mother was human.

After listening to over a dozen tracks he walked out of the store a satisfied customer. He had found a group called Muscles of Green who sounded pretty good by his standards. His grin slowly faded as he hit the streets of the downtown area, nearly walking smack into the middle of the riots that had already started with laser fire streaking across the intersection.

Relliants and street hoodlums went about destroying property as a result of their melee, pedestrians caught in the crossfire. The same scene greeted him about a mile down when he turned on a familiar street that was a short cut to his apartment.

As he got into the elevator of his building he looked at his watch and saw the time at 7:45. He had a mission to do at 8:30 and needed to hurry or be late. Entering the foyer of his apartment and throwing his purchase on the sofa, he headed straight for the bed- room closet to flip through his arsenal of clothes. For his small effort of rummaging he came across a green and black dinner dress.

"Perfect," he said to himself.

He dropped the dress on the bed and went into the bathroom, shifting into a female form. Twenty minutes later she came out brushing her hair then twisted it back, securing it with a hair clip of black design. She smiled at herself naked in the mirror and laughed.

"You are gorgeous."

She slipped on the dress and matching heels. Entering the den, she picked up her small laser gun and dropped it in the purse, slinging it over her shoulder. A tiny cylinder about an inch long went on her inner thigh under her dress. Now she was ready.

A horn blew from under her window, signaling that the limo had arrived. She took her time going down and as she approached the car, the passenger door was opened for her by the driver. She slithered in wearing her most winning smile and addressed the man inside wearing a tuxedo.

"Senator, you look smashing."

Being a telepath as well, the changer saw him smile back at her while thinking how wrong his aide was in saying that she was dangerous. His thoughts were loud in her head.

'If anything, she'll screw my brains out and give me a heart attack.'

She just kept a grin on her face as she thought. *Not quite, Senator.*

Of course it was the usual conspiracy theory and a light assignment but it still had to be done.

The Senator did not want Relliants on the planet surface.

The Senator felt dinner was fine but dessert would be better. He could have eaten her alive in the limo except for the fact it would have been tacky on his part. Still, he restrained himself in the hotel room he had picked specifically for its privacy and the view, overlooking the harbor.

At a towering 6'8" tall with just the right amount of muscles to match, the Senator was a huge man with what he felt was an awesome physique. He reportedly had the most perfect body in town. His curly brown hair, a touch of grey on the temples, fell to his shoulders and was always combed away from his face to show off his soft dark eyes and perfectly shaped mouth. Features close to being Relliant. The Senator also had a plan but it entailed something entirely different than what the changer was plotting.

"Come to daddy, baby."

He motioned for her to come closer. She moved forward, undressing as she did so, her breast barely moving, making him wince at the splendid curves of her body and well-built leg muscles. Her smile made her look luscious-good enough to eat. To the Senator's amazement, as she came closer, her dress dropped to the floor and a laser gun was aimed at him set for kill. By its strange design he could tell it was Relliant.

"I don't think so, Senator."

Leveling the gun, ready to fire, she felt a sudden pain in her hands. The laser gun was gone and she herself was on the floor with the Senator towering over her, his eyes black as night. She groped for the cylinder and her touch activated it. Light shot from both ends of the device as she got to her feet and spun it with deadly force.

The Senator laughed while charging towards the changer, the move shocking her. Instinct kicked in and she had him down on the carpet straddling him. She was about to deliver the final blow when he grabbed her by the hair, flipping her over. Using his powerful legs, he kept her pinned as he leaned down to smell her flesh.

"I know who you are, what you are, and why you are here. I thought we could have some fun first but I see you didn't have that in mind. Then again, you didn't do your homework."

"What are you talking about?" The changer yelled through gritted teeth.

The Senator undid his trousers and pushed them down far enough for her to see the overlarge genitalia with its scale like shell and absence of testicles.

"No!" she screamed in disbelief. "You can't be!"

"I've been hungry since we left the restaurant. Human food does nothing for me. Too bad. You would have made a great lay but you'll make an even better toy to desecrate."

The Senator moistened his lips and drove his oversized sex organ into her, shredding flesh in the process. He sank his teeth into her shoulder to take a big chunk in his mouth then continued to devour her alive.

◆◆◆

While the remains of his dinner companion were being cleared away, the Senator sat in the lobby. His aide had arrived shortly after being called and before the police came to question the maid who'd gone into the room to find it painted red with blood. The aide began to rant out loud about the whole situation.

"I knew there was something bad in the air! Are we going to have to contact next of kin?"

"No," the Senator replied softly, "She was an assassin."

"Relliant?" His aide asked quietly. The Senator nodded. "Does anyone know?"

"Know what?"

"That you are a Senigranke?"

"Of course not. The Relliance can do whatever they want to try and kill me because it will never happen."

"You are half Relliant, Senator."

"But I am far more sinister and powerful than those mediocre creatures."

The aide sighed heavily.

"Shall I fetch you a late snack?"

"Oh, yes, thank you," the Senator smiled and added, "Make sure it's a male this time."

"As you wish, sir."

THE LAST IN LINE....

SANCTUARY

The underground cavern was so silent even air seemed to barely move within it. Drops of condensation echoed as they hit the cold stone floor, disrupting the void. Two teenage boys descended slowly down the slippery stone stairway, careful not to settle the weight of their feet on any broken steps. They only had one job to do; awaken an entity deep in slumber within the cave. Their master demanded it. He had lost sight of his prey who had become trapped inside and needed to flush him out into the open. It seemed a lot of work for a single human enigma, but their master's orders were absolute.

As they reached the landing at the bottom, the cold dampness sent shivers through their very bones. Off to the left was the drum set that had been brought down ahead of time. The red haired boy sat down at it while the dark haired boy stood near the wall by the stairwell ready to run if needed. They had both been warned about the entity waking up and possibly mistaking them as targets.

Picking up the drumsticks, the red head glanced over at the other boy.

"Call it," the dark haired one whispered. He set one foot on the first step.

The red head boy's brow furrowed and beads of sweat began to form while he beat on the single snare drum, his right foot hitting the bass drum below in slow successions. A soft blue glowed from his eyes. His friend backed further against the wall and took another step up. The sound of stones breaking apart and falling like an avalanche filled the area. A breeze swept through the cave, turning into a gust of wind as a bright blue haze of light filled with electricity sped past them.

The dark haired boy waited until the red head had abandoned the drum set, then both of them ran up the stairs in fear. Halfway up, he spoke.

"That should get him out of here."

His eyes glowed blue for a brief second.

◆◆◆

Charlie had been running for his life for days and hoped his legs were still strong enough to outrun whatever was coming after him. He had ended up in an underground cave whose layout was like a labyrinth. There was no sense of time down there and he imagined he had been trapped in it for at least a day. He heard drums earlier and what sounded like parts of the cave collapsing, but figured he was just losing his mind.

Now something else chased him, steering him through the maze and coming up fast. Against his better judgment he looked back to see what it was. He wished he hadn't. A skull the size of a boulder sped towards him in midair, blue light shooting out of its sockets. The sound emitting from it was hideous and made his insides feel like jelly. Sharp blasts of hot air came from its gaping mouth, whipping Charlie's hair into his eyes but he paid no mind. There was light at the end of the passageway which meant a way out.

The sight of the trees almost made Charlie smile as he stepped out onto the grass but his hopes shattered like glass. A group dressed in dark, hooded robes surrounded the opening above ground in a semi-circle around the cave's entrance.

His eyes went wide as one of them pointed to him and announced, "This is Charlie."

Charlie heard his own blood curdling scream as he realized he was trapped with the skull behind him and the hooded beings before him. Darkness folded over him.

Charlie saw hands grip a shopping cart handle in front of him and snapped out of his state of doom. Taking in his surroundings he found himself in the cookie and crackers aisle of a grocery store;

And in the form of a woman.

It's happened again!

Out of sheer fright, she had not only teleported herself out of that situation but shifted gender as well. It was not something that Charlie could completely control just yet. Feeling safe for now in a different scenario, she took a deep breath to calm herself.

In the cave she had been wearing a black body tunic. Now she wore a full length cream and brown wool coat, black turtle neck dress and black boots. People stared as they walked past her because she was standing in the middle of the store with a look of horror frozen on her face. She decided to act natural and pretend to do a little shopping.

Her mind was still in a state of confusion as Charlie mindlessly grabbed items off the shelf, tossing them into the cart. In the canned goods aisle reaching for a fruit cocktail, she felt a presence.

A kind of light buzzing filled her head, making the hair on her body seem to rise up. Some ambiguous yet unfriendly feeling. Not daring to turn around she put the can in the cart and got ready to push it forward. A pale hand, larger than her own clamped on top of hers, stopping the cart from moving, and a man's voice whispered in her ear.

"Did you really think you could get away from me Charlie?"

She turned and saw a man with pale skin dressed entirely in black and eyes of the same color devoid of white. The smile on his face conveyed nothing nice.

"What do you want from me?" She cried softly.

Her hands gripped the cart handle tighter.

"I want your life-force," the man in black whispered. "I want your soul." His black eyes glowed blue like the rolling skull in the cave.

"No!"

Charlie backed away but stopped as people started screaming.

The man in the black suit just laughed as he stepped away from her. She was pushed aside by a group of shoppers running towards the double doors.

Determined to be rid of the evil pursuing her, she ran to the doors along with the crowd. Some fell and were trampled by the stampede pushing their way out. Charlie could not seem to get any closer to escaping with them. When only a few stragglers were left still in the store ready to flee, they suddenly stopped and parted like the red sea. Two people held the doors open and she saw what was in store for her.

A tidal wave of water, dirt and dead leaves flowed into the store, pushing her body back into the store. The coat weighed her down as it engulfed her, the sludge filling her mouth. Shelves were tossed out of the way creating a path to the warehouse. It churned through the dock doors carrying her down the hill behind the store, burrowing underground. The last thought Charlie had before losing consciousness was that this is where she would be kept until the evil thing needed her.

◆◆◆

Charlie was tired, hungry and scared. After forcing her body to listen to her pleas and teleport out of the muddy prison, she had awakened on the side of a road in nothing but a bra and panties. The dark of night greeted her along with rain that had soaked her to the bone, leaving her skin pale as she walked slowly on shaky legs.

She had no idea how long she'd been buried. The state of her body offered a clue. Her former athletic body was now a few pounds short of emaciation, her limbs felt weak and a steady nausea kept her equilibrium off. It took everything she had to move, let alone walk and it also meant reverting back to male form was not an option for a while.

A house came into view a few miles away but she doubted making it that far. Her legs were on the verge of giving up and she had little energy left. With labored breathing she stopped and scanned the area along the paved road in the middle of nowhere. Nothing except grass on either side of her and the only light came from the house ahead. Having no choice but to resolve herself to reach it, she trudged forward, step by step in what seemed like a lifetime, until she miraculously stood at the opened front gates inviting her in.

Overgrown foliage cascaded along the walkway from the rusty, iron front gates right up to the stoned porch. A dark, heavy metal sign nearly strangled by vines, tilted at a forty five degree angle with bronze lettering, read

'SANCTUARY'

Charlie smirked in disgust. This was as much of a sanctuary as the cavern or that rundown grocery store and had to be a trap. But, right now, Charlie needed rest in order to fight another day. Trudging up the weed clogged walkway that scraped her bare feet, she fell onto the door and lifted the heavy knocker, banging three times.

Seconds felt like eternity before an overhead light came on as the door wheezed open. As it widened, she fell forward right into the foyer without shame or grace. A tall lanky man in a black suit carrying a candelabra leaned over her. A glimpse at a wooden spiral staircase on her right, she noticed it matched the wooden floor she lay on. With one arm, the man picked her up and threw her over his shoulder. She didn't get to see anything else because she passed out from exhaustion.

◆◆◆

I have to get out!

Charlie screamed inside her head as her fingers clawed air before realizing she was no longer in that muddy grave. Opening her eyes, she found herself lying on a giant bed in an equally large room. Save for the yellow glow of light coming from under the doorway it was dark. Her vision was blurry and she couldn't make out much of her surroundings. The only other piece of furniture was a nightstand that held a glass of water. At first the glass appeared to have a light blue hazy glow, but then faded away.

Lifting her head off the pillow she instinctively placed a hand on her chest to confirm she was still female, even though she knew her body had no energy to change back so soon. Reaching for the glass her hand shook uncontrollably. A dark figure appeared next to the bed and gently held her head up, tilting the glass to her lips.

She choked on the second sip and the glass was lowered. Her eyes adjusted to the darkness, making out a suit jacket and white shirt, and recognized the tall man who had carried her like a sack of meal.

"Easy girl," he whispered softly. He let her drink a little more then set the glass back on the nightstand. "You seem to have been in quite an ordeal."

He tucked her back in under the covers. Charlie tried to speak but her vocal chords wouldn't obey. The man somehow sensed this and laid a hand on her forehead to stop her from moving.

"Shh," he cooed softly. "Not yet."

Charlie felt her body get heavy and began drifting off into a deep sleep. The last thing that went through her mind was, *'that wasn't just water'*.

Awake again and Charlie was still feeling a bit shaky though nothing like before. This time she was able to sit up and observe the room. The air smelled of old wood and the overhead lighting did nothing to penetrate the gloom. Layers of grey and black sheer curtains covered the picture window to her right blocking her ability to tell the time of day.

The door opened and the tall man stood illuminated by the hall light with a tray held up by his finger- tips. Squinting, she could make out a small sandwich and a small dish of mixed fruit. His blank expression made her cringe as he strode across the room, setting the tray on the nightstand. Charlie licked her cracked lips with a dry tongue. A new glass of clear liquid was already next to her.

"Where am I?"

Her voice croaked when she asked.

"Sanctuary," he replied.

"What is that?" She nodded at the glass.

"A mild sedative."

"Can I have just plain old water?"

"Of course."

He left the room, coming back moments later with a blue glass.

"Thank you."

Charlie took the water from him and gulped it down, making sure the liquid also touched her lips. He retrieved the empty glass and set the tray on her lap. A soft grumbling noise erupted from her belly signaling hunger.

She shoved the sandwich in her mouth and chewed loudly, glancing warily at the man who stood motionless at her side. When she was done chewing, the fruit was next. Picking up the dish, she chucked its contents into her mouth, doing the same. With a gulp the last of it went down.

The glass of sedative was waiting for her in his hand as he held it in front of her. She stared at it for a long time then looked up at him. There was still no expression on his face but she knew he was not leaving until she drank at least half of it.

So I'm going to be held captive drugged.

She took the glass and obeyed the silent command.

It hit her almost instantly, causing her to fall back heavily down on the pillow. Her vision blurred and the room tilted. The tall man set the glass on the tray and exited the room. Darkness enclosed her world once again.

◆◆◆

"Good evening, miss. Are you feeling well today?" A female voice from close by asked.

Charlie struggled to open her eyes and when they did, she saw a woman in a maid uniform yank the curtains open letting the light of the setting sun filter in. Her head felt like a ton of lead but she managed to lift it along with the rest of her upper body. On raised elbows, she scanned the room in the weak light and noticed a closet on the opposite side.

"Fine, I guess." She licked her lips and winced at the stinging pain.

The maid went to the closet and flung open its doors. An array of dresses lined the hanging rod. She perused the selections until she found one that appeared to suit her tastes. Charlie saw the maid's pick and grimaced. The woman turned to her and smiled.

"This should work for supper."

'No it doesn't', Charlie wanted to shout as the maid laid out the cream colored frilly dress on the foot of the bed. She reached over and touched the fabric and was surprised at how soft it felt. Still, it was definitely a throwback to an older era.

"I'll be back to fetch you in half an hour. Please be dressed and ready to come down."

As the maid left, Charlie leaned forward and crept to the edge of the foot board. She leaned over to inspect the floor which appeared to swirl around until settling on old dark wooden planks.

The drugs?

She sat back on her knees and waited for her equilibrium to stabilize.

It finally dawned on her that she was indeed naked and certainly wasn't when she arrived. Luckily, she didn't have much to look at so going sans underwear was not a problem. Dragging the dress to her, she found it hard to put on because her entire body ached. Every muscle pulled taut as she stretched to get it over her head.

She swung her legs over the edge to test her footing on the floor. The first time she stood up straight, her balance faltered and she fell back on the bed. Taking a few deep breaths, she tried again and was successful with small steps across the room.

The door swung open and the maid stood smiling, waiting. Half an hour had passed already. Just to see how far the rabbit hole went, she walked up to the woman.

"What is the name of this place?"

"Why, this is Sanctuary." The maid smiled sweetly. "Come, this way."

Charlie obediently followed her down the hall. As soon as she regained a little more strength, she was getting out of here.

The dining room was gloomy with incandescent bulbs casting an eerie orange light causing the food on the table to look unappetizing at best but the quality could be seen. Roast duck, cranberry chutney and what appeared to be a creamed rice, (*or was it gnocchi?*), ran down the middle of the long table. Four other people sat waiting patiently for the food to be served. A chair was pulled out for Charlie and as she sat, was pushed towards the table.

No one looked up to acknowledge her as the newcomer and it made her nervous. They couldn't care less; this was a normal affair. Old dark wood armoires lined the walls and she could make out knick knacks and china ware. In front of her was a plain white china saucer and wide bowl. Scanning the table, she didn't see anything requiring a bowl.

As if on cue, the maid arrived pushing a metal cart holding a large white serving dish. She stopped at every person and ladled steaming brown liquid into the bowls. When she came around to Charlie's, she easily identified it as French onion soup.

The main vegetable was sliced to thin perfection and swirled in the broth. Charlie's stomach made a whiny gurgle, causing the other guests to look up from their raised spoons positioned at mouth height.

"So sorry," Charlie whispered. "Haven't eaten much in a while."

The guests went back to focusing on their soup and in unison sipped from their spoons. A lack of interest in her was obvious. Charlie lifted her spoon and tried a sip of the soup. To her amazement, it was probably the best soup she had ever had in her life. Trying not to seem greedy, she methodically finished her bowl at the same time as the others.

With lightning speed, the tall man, obviously the butler, removed the bowls and whisked them away though double doors in the corner of the room. Charlie sat stunned by the quick movement even as the maid began cutting the roast duck, placing a slice on each saucer. Apparently, no one was faze by it.

What the hell was that?

There was no reason for such quick action. She thought dinner was supposed to be enjoyed at a leisurely pace. Using large spoons, the maid put one spoonful of chutney and the creamy starch on each plate. After she was done, there was no remaining food in the serving dishes and with the help of the butler, they were swiftly cleared away. Once the two disappeared behind the double doors, the guests commenced eating.

In deafening silence they all ate. An occasional clank of silverware against china was heard along with chewing. It had the feelings of a last meal and Charlie wondered if this was going to be hers. A glimmer of something blue swept past the corner of her eye and she looked up towards one of the male guests across from her to the left. He patted the edge of his mouth with his napkin.

Am I seeing things?'

The man was not doing anything out of the ordinary as far as she could tell.

With the meal done, the butler came and did his super speed bussing of the table. Each guest stood up as their place was cleared and Charlie did the same. They all turned and exited the dining room but the maid stopped her in the hallway.

"I will escort you back to your room."

"What, no dessert?" Charlie quipped.

"Not tonight. Only on the weekends."

Charlie made a mental note of this.

So, it wasn't a weekend, but what day was it?

She decided asking now would be pushing it. At least she knew it was nighttime. Maybe in the middle of the night she could gauge the time more accurately by looking at the moon.

Back in her gloomy bedroom, Charlie noticed a white nightgown laid across the foot of the bed and sighed at its plainness then caught herself. What did she care about fashion or clothes? Even in her male form, that was not a dire issue. To her chagrin, the maid stood and waited for her to undress and put it on. The frilly dinner dress was taken from her and draped across the maid's arm.

Charlie climbed back in bed and was startled as the butler set a glass in her hand when she settled into a sitting position.

When did he come in?

She stared at the glass then grasped it tighter.

"A nightcap for you," the maid explained and left the room.

The butler stood still, waiting. Charlie took another look at the glass and checked the consistency. Its movements suggested a liquid other than water.

Another drugging.

She eyed the butler and didn't her stare waver as she downed it. Handing the empty glass back to him, she slid down under the covers and watched him leave. Her plan to check the moonlight was derailed for now.

Six days.

Charlie had determined that it was Tuesday by her calculations since the last dessert day was two days ago. The nightly drugging had stopped after three days and she wasn't sure if it meant they didn't see her as a threat or something was coming. Her gut screamed 'be careful!' Since her arrival two of the guests had left and three new ones had taken their place. She was sure to meet them at 'supper' tonight.

Who says that anymore?

During the day she was allowed to sit in the lounge that had a library of old books. Sometimes she wandered the halls to try and gauge the layout of the house. Whenever she ventured too far away from the dining area or the lounge, the butler would appear to escort her back. Each day was boring and uneventful. She had tried to start a conversation with a few of the other guests in the lounge but they never acknowledged her. One man even got up and moved to the other side of the room on one particular occasion.

Her plan for tonight was to shift back into male form and find a way out. She had figured out from the last shifting how her body reacted during the transition and was able to recreate it. All those days of resting had reenergized her body and she felt ready for battle.

The first exit to try would be the front door. If that didn't work then she would have to take some chances while scoping out the place for another. She had already stolen some men's attire from the other male guests' closets while they were out and hidden them in the back of her own closet.

The maid and butler didn't seem to care about securing guests' clothes because they belonged to the house. She figured each guest was assigned a room based on gender. That was the only explanation for her closet having just female garments.

On cue, the bedroom door swung open and the maid appeared to peruse the closet for yet another awful dress reminiscent of the early twentieth century circa 1910. Charlie was always amazed by how the clothes weren't riddled with moth damage.

Turning back from the closet, the maid smiled holding out a powder green lace covered thing that seemed a tad too long. Charlie put it on and sure enough it fell to the floor forming a two inch train behind her. She looked up and seeing pure delight on the maid's face knew some gaudy matching head band was next.

Suppertime, as always, was just the right touch of gloomy. Charlie mimicked the natives patiently waiting to be served. There were six guests total now, herself included, and they were seated three to each side of the long table. Cream of mushroom soup was the first course. Charlie savored its delicate flavors with every spoonful.

A glimmer caught her eye, this time she was sure it was blue. Every meal time it happened and she still had no idea where it came from. But tonight no speculation needed. Sitting across from her to the left was a tall man with shoulder length dark hair. Not just dark, but pitch black, the color of night. His black suit and tie were tailored to his body. What made her mouth open wide in an 'O' was his sinister smile and the bright blue glowing eyes that stared back at her.

Charlie's hand started to shake and she gripped her fork hard trying to stop it. She could feel tears stinging behind her eyes and willed them back. His eyes stopped glowing, returned to black pupils, to her relief with whites. She realized he had continued eating along with the other guests while she sat stunned, immobile. Fearing scrutiny, she made up time and caught up with them before the butler or maid came back.

As the guests filed out of the dining room, the man slowed down his stride to walk beside her and deeply breathe in her scent.

"I won't let you go, Charlie," he whispered in her ear before turning down the opposite way of the corridor.

Charlie's body shivered with terror, remembering where she had been before coming to the house. That muddy grave he trapped her in to suck every bit of life force from her was waiting. The maid came smiling to escort her back to the dank bedroom and Charlie knew with conviction that this was the night to flee.

◆◆◆

Two hours after being alone in the room, Charlie shifted back into male form and donned the dark slacks and white undershirt. The shoes were a size too small but at least he could run in them if necessary. On a whim he decided to grab the dark button down shirt as well, leaving it undone. Ruffling his hair, he carefully opened the bedroom door and eased out into the corridor.

The house was dark and silent as a tomb. Charlie wondered what the rest of the occupants were doing. Off in the distance, he saw a flicker of candle light and headed towards it as swiftly as possible without making much noise. He came to the foyer of the front door and let out a lungful of air before gripping the handle.

Swinging it open, ready to run, he was stopped short; left gaping at the scene in front of him.

Beyond the threshold of the front porch lay a landscape of otherworldly design. Dark purple sky filled the horizon and even darker shapes crept along the ground leaving trails. Strange green trees, stripped of leaves, bowed down at the command of a strong wind coursing through the air. One of the dark shapes slowed its slither and turned its head towards Charlie. Electric blue eyes glowed menacingly at him.

Charlie slammed the front door shut.

For what seemed like an eternity, he stood still at the door, trying to get his breathing under control. Beads of sweat formed along his forehead and he could feel his hands shaking. That someone may have heard the door slam dawned on him, forcing his body to move quickly out of sight. Looking around in the half light of the candles, he saw corridors that he had never seen the guests venture along. Picking one at random, Charlie headed down it.

After passing at least ten doors, Charlie's curiosity got the better of him and he slowly turned the knob of one, easing it open. There was a bedroom very similar to the one he had been staying in. Just as he was about to close the door, the far wall lit up filling the room with bright light and a man emerged. He seemed weary with splotches of red all over his clothes and body. The smell confirmed it was blood; human blood. His icy blue eyes dimmed to a dark hue and he fell onto the bed unconscious.

"Oh dear," the maid's voice called from behind. "Looks like another one is in need of care."

Charlie stood paralyzed with fear as the maid walked past him into the room and began tending to the new guest. He slowly backed away and his feet sped up until he was half running further down the corridor. At a dead end he made a left and continued until it too ended. This time, there was a door. With shaky hands, he gripped the handle and pushed.

A room of pure white lay before him. Everything inside was the same color, blending together to the point where he couldn't quite make out where the furniture began and ended. One thing he did know; its presence smacked of pure evil intent. His skin prickled and the hairs on his body stood on end. There was no one in the room yet he could hear whispers. The picture window looked out to a vast darkness, tiny lights like stars shining within it.

Charlie backed out of that room as well, shutting the door. He ran down the corridor from which he came and went the opposite way at the first dead end.

In the middle of another hallway he stopped to take a deep breath.

What am I doing?

He shook his head to clear it and looked at the wall straight ahead. Charlie closed his eyes and concentrated on his surroundings, pinpointing every room in the house then began teleporting to them one by one. All of the rooms on the second and third floor were pure white. From the outside, the house was two stories.

How many floors are inside this thing?

He was a third of the way into it when he caught a glimpse of something close by in one of the rooms.

"Mmm, Charlie. Be careful," a deep male voice cooed at him.

Charlie turned to his left and out of the room's wall came his nemesis striding out of a pool of darkness. He still wore the black suit from dinner, hands shoved deep in his pants' front pockets, and stopped about ten feet from him.

"I wouldn't want you to get lost. I need you."

He smiled again.

Screaming filled the air and Charlie found it was coming from himself as he fled from the room, teleporting to another. He continued his investigation, spurred by desperation, and by his count there were 200 rooms inside the decrepit mansion.

"One of these has to be the way out," he said softly to himself.

An idea finally came to him why the man might be hunting him and Charlie berated himself for not noticing it sooner. Maybe it had something to do with the strange powers he possessed. He had no memories of his life before the chase began some months ago but never thought to try and figure it out. That said, he wasn't going to just hand himself over all gift wrapped.

He teleported to a room on the second floor close the end of the house and hurried in. Standing in front of the far wall he loudly exhaled twice and after the second pursed his lips along with a small sniff. Without hesitation he hurled himself towards it and passed through.

Red.

Blood dripped, covering everything. The walls, the ceiling, the floor, all a sticky mess. His nostrils whiffed a smell like no other and he gagged, nearly retching. A glance to his right made him regret looking around for the reason because he found it. What was left of human remains were piled high in a mound and one of the dark shadow creatures he had seen at the front door was shoveling some of it up.

Before he could scream or vomit, a hand clamped over his mouth and the man in black's hot breath caressed his ear.

"No, no, Charlie. This is no place for you to be. You were safer in the warm grave I made for you." He said softly as he dragged Charlie out of that bloody plane and back into the white room.

Charlie struggled but could not get away from the man who was nearly twice his size. In desperation, he mindlessly teleported to the fifth floor and overshot his calculations of the hallway. He ended up in yet another white room.

There he fell to his knees and the amazing dinner emptied out of him in waves. Spitting out the last of it, he wiped his mouth with the back of his hand and felt the tears burning his eyes stream down his face.

He slammed a fist on the floor and forced himself to stand up.

Not yet.

He wasn't going to give up so soon. Taking a few deep breaths, he scanned the room. It felt cold. Even the picture window looked out onto a white surface yet he climbed through it.

Giant rodents combed the area and Charlie fell backwards on his butt. He was never one to be afraid of rats but when one the size of a car sauntered past him, giving him a disinterested look with red eyes, he became so. Further in, he saw half an arm and partial legs dangling from the mouth of another. Knowing there was no food left in his stomach, he still tasted bile.

Off in the distance, a curly haired blonde and an Asian man were battling the giant beasts. The Asian beheaded one while the blonde sliced another in half. As both slid backwards past him, he was sprayed with the blood of rats. He joined the men heading for the exit and leaped back through the window, landing hard on the room floor. They rolled to a stop.

"Let's go!"

The Asian commanded breathing hard.

Confused, Charlie sat up and stared at him. Then the blonde grabbed him by the shirt collar and hauled him up towards the door. The head of a giant rat emerged from the window, then two more. His eyes went wide as he realized they were coming for them. Charlie did not need any more persuasion.

At the door, the blonde was able to stab the first rat in the eye before they got into the hallway and the Asian slammed the door shut. Charlie looked at the two men covered in blood and out of breath.

Friend or Foe? He asked himself.

The fading blue light of their eyes gave him a clue.

"At least we made it," The blonde rasped. "I could use some rest," The Asian agreed.

The two men stood up and brushed themselves off the best they could. Charlie watched them wipe their weapons on their clothes and then wander off down the hall.

Dazed, he tried to wrap his head around what just happened.

Giant rats? Piles of body parts?

Had he stumbled into some sort of drug induced vortex?

Drug induced?

"No, no, no, no, no!" Charlie yelled holding his head.

He stood straight and frantically looked around him. With an even stronger conviction to be free, he teleported again.

The room was three times larger than all the others and so purely white that it hurt Charlie's eyes. Evil poured out of the walls and into every pore making his whole body feel like gelatin as he slumped to the floor. Multilayered whispers surrounded him, rising in decibel level. He clamped his hands over his ears to block out the sounds but to no avail.

"Oh, you are so special," the voices sighed around him. "So pure and full of energy."

Charlie raised his head and his eyes widened.

What?

His hands shook.

"We need more of you. You must stay."

The breathy words vibrated the room.

"Let me out!" Charlie cried out, his despair on full display.

"No," a deep male voice replied.

It was so close to him that, although he knew who it was, Charlie turned to see.

◆◆◆

The soup spoon made a loud clang against the bowl as Charlie's grip loosened. Head spinning, he tried to adjust his fuzzy vision and saw the frilly lace cuffs around his wrists. His eyes trailing upwards, Charlie realized he was back in female form at the dinner table.

A wave of panic emerged.

Across the table from Charlie sat the man who had given chase for all tis time. He had a smile of satisfaction on his face and his blue gaze never wavered from while he slowly sipped from his soup spoon.

She could feel the tears wet and stingy. Defeated, she began to cry, letting them fall into her soup.

"None of that, my dear," he chided. "I decided you would better serve me this way than sucking the life energy out of you."

"Why?" Charlie whispered.

"You're wrong. You're not a demon like us, but something more pure and celestial." Charlie looked up at him in shock. "Yes, we demons always have a hard time capturing one of your kind but when we do, the rush is," he sighed and took a deep breath, "Exhilarating."

"We're nothing but food, then," Charlie spat.

"Mmm, not so much food but fuel. In any case, you are mine now."

"I don't understand."

"A hybrid of our kind and yours is something we never considered, until now." He smiled again seeing Charlie turn ill. "Since you were my prey, it is only fair that you become mine."

"I won't," Charlie stuttered in horror. "I would never submit to you."

"Not to worry," the demon laughed as he set his spoon down. "I took the liberty of consummating our bond while you were recuperating."

Charlie covered her mouth with one hand and held herself up on the table with the other. Her mind had been under the influence of drugs the whole time since the third day. She stared into his evil eyes brimming with pride as the maid came around to clear the bowls.

"What is this place?" Charlie cried softly, asking no one.

"Why, this is Sanctuary," the maid answered in her cheery voice.

"For demons," the man added. He reached over to wipe a tear from Charlie's face.

~END~

ABOUT THE AUTHOR

I had a passion for the written word since age seven, reading everything I could get my grubby hands on which included encyclopedias and the thesaurus. At twelve, I had my first encounter with a Stephen King novel and was hooked. Since I was a huge horror and science fiction fan the contents were right up my alley. It inspired me to write my own brand of fiction, combining multiple genres to keep things interesting.

Always ready to learn new things, my search for knowledge never ceases. I currently have two degrees: Accounting and Business Administration, was a certified Nail Technician and studied Digital Film and Video for two years at the Art Institute of Portland.

Anime is my drug of choice, and I frequent Cons to immerse myself in geekdom. I also love a great bottle of wine and rock out to heavy metal music.

Like me on Facebook and Twitter:
@Maquel AJ1

Look me up on Goodreads

Track MAJart Works on Instagram

AND CHECK OUT THE WEBSITES

WWW.MAQUELAJACOB.COM

WWW.MAJARTWORKS.COM